In peace I will lie down
and sleep. Lord, you
alone keep me safe.

PSALM 4:8 NIRV

New Growth Press, Greensboro, NC 27404
www.newgrowthpress.com
Text copyright © 2019 by George Thomas (Champ) Thornton, II
Illustration copyright © 2019 by Rommel Ruiz

Cover and interior illustration: Rommel Ruiz, rommelruiz.com
Title treatment: Nathan Douglas Yoder

ISBN: 978-1-64507-030-6

Library of Congress Control Number: 2019945033


Printed in Canada

26 25 24 23 22 21 20 19      2 3 4 5 6

# WHY DO WE SAY Good Night?

CHAMP
THORNTON

Illustrated by
ROMMEL RUIZ

When nighttime comes
and no more light,
you get in bed;
we say *good night*.

But when it's dark,
and I can't see—
Why do you say
good night to me?

It's not the same
when there's no light.
The dark's not good.
I don't like night.

I'm glad you told
me how you feel.
But stop to think,
What else is real?

The Lord made day.
The Lord made night.
So even dark
is good and right.

But you can't see when
dark surrounds.
What is that shape?
What is that sound?

Yet God sees all;
his sight's not dim.
The dark is like
bright light to him.

So when it's dark—
with perfect sight—
our God is watching
through the night.

Yes, God can see
when you're in bed,
when scary thoughts
run through your head.

But there is more
for you to hear:
We say good night
'cause God is near.

Just like a shepherd
guards his sheep,
the Lord protects
when we're asleep.

Please help me, Lord,
to trust in you—
for all you are
and all you do.

Lord, you made night,
and you can see.
You're the Shepherd
who cares for me.

Since God is with
you in the night,

Since he made nighttime
good and right,

Since God can see
without the light . . .

All this
is why

we say
*good night.*

Good night, dear one—
You need not fear.

Good night, sleep well.
The Lord is here . . .

Good night.